HUCKLEBERRY FINN

HUCKLEBERRY FINN
By Mark Twain

Adapted by June Edwards
Illustrated by Sherry Neidigh

RSVP
**RAINTREE
STECK-VAUGHN**
PUBLISHERS
The Steck-Vaughn Company

Austin, Texas

Copyright © 1991 Steck-Vaughn Company

Copyright © 1980 Raintree Publishers Limited Partnership

Library of Congress Number: 79-24312

Library of Congress Cataloging-in-Publication Data

Edwards, June.
　Huckleberry Finn.

　SUMMARY: A 19th-century boy, floating down the Mississippi River on a raft with a runaway slave, becomes involved with a feuding family, two scoundrels pretending to be royalty, and Tom Sawyer's aunt, who mistakes him for Tom.
　[1. Mississippi River—Fiction. 2. Missouri—Fiction] I. Neidigh, Sherry. II. Clemens, Samuel Langhorne, 1835-1910. Adventures of Huckleberry Finn. III. Title.
PZ7.E2563Hu　　[Fic.]　　79-24312

ISBN 0-8172-1651-0 hardcover library binding

ISBN 0-8114-6826-7 softcover binding

18 19 20 21 22 23　99 98 97 96 95 94

CONTENTS

THE ROBBER BAND

1

A twig snapped in the dark among the trees. Huckleberry sat on his bed on the second floor and listened.

"Me-yow. Me-yow!" he heard.

Huck climbed out the window and onto the shed roof. He jumped to the ground and ran toward the trees where his friend, Tom Sawyer, was waiting.

Huckleberry knew the Widow Douglas would be very upset about his sneaking out. He had no mother and had lived with his drunkard father until last year. He slept on doorsteps and never went to school or church. His days were spent fishing and swimming. When his father disappeared, the Widow Douglas took Huck into her home and treated him like a son. Huckleberry liked her, but he had to wear tight clothes that made him sweat. He had to come to supper on time, say prayers before meals, and learn about the Bible. Sometimes Huck had to get away and run free again.

After Huck found Tom, the two friends raced to the hill at the edge of town. They lay in the weeds and watched the lights shining in the far-off windows. Soon other boys joined them.

"You gotta swear to keep a secret," whispered Tom.

"I swear," said Huckleberry and the others.

"Then follow me," answered Tom.

The boys climbed the bank to a clump of bushes. In the middle was a large hole hidden by leaves. They lit candles and crawled on their hands and knees through a passage-way to a small cave in the hillside. It was damp and cold inside. The boys sat close together to keep warm.

"We're gonna be a band of robbers," said Tom Sawyer. "We each have to take an oath and write our names in blood."

Huckleberry shivered with excitement. Tom wrote the oath on a big sheet of paper. Each boy must swear to tell no secrets. If he did anything bad to another member, he would be killed. A big cross would be cut across his chest, the sign of the band. His throat would be cut and his body burned. His name would be marked off the list with blood and a curse would be on him forever.

"That's a wonderful oath," said Ben Rogers. "Did you think it up yourself?"

"Most of it," said Tom proudly, "but part came out of robber books. Every high-class robber gang has an oath like this." It was beautiful, the boys agreed. They wished they were as smart as Tom.

"I think if a boy tells a secret we should kill his family, too," said one of the boys.

"That's a good idea," replied Tom. He took his pencil and added that to the paper.

"What about Huckleberry?" asked Ben. "He ain't got no family."

"Ain't he got a father?" asked Tom.

"Yeah, but you can't ever find him. He ain't been seen around here for over a year."

The boys decided that Huck would have to be dropped from the band. Everybody had to have a family to kill or it would not be fair. Huckleberry hung his head in shame. Then he had a bright idea.

"What about Miss Watson?" he asked. Miss Watson was the sister of the Widow Douglas. She had recently come to live with them and was always saying things like, "Don't put your feet up there, Huckleberry. Sit up straight, Huckleberry." She also made him work an hour every

night on his spelling. The boys agreed that Miss Watson would do and Huckleberry was back in the gang.

"Now," said Ben Rogers, "what are we gonna do?"

"Why, robbery and murder," said Tom. "We'll be highwaymen. We'll stop stagecoaches on the road and kill the people and take their watches and money and stuff."

"Do we have to kill the women, too?" asked Ben fearfully.

"No, of course not. You're so dumb, Ben," said Tom. "You take the women to the cave and are real nice to them. Then they fall in love with you and never want to go home again."

"Well, all right, but I don't like it much," said Ben. "We'll have the cave so full of women there won't be any place for the robbers."

Tom Sawyer was chosen head of the gang and the boys started for home. Huckleberry climbed up the shed and into his bedroom window just as the sun came up. His new clothes were muddy, but he was too tired to care. He felt very proud to be a member of such an important band.

The boys played highwaymen for about a month. They ran out of the woods at hog drivers and women taking vegetables to the market. They never did kill anyone. All they stole were doughnuts from a Sunday School picnic.

Huckleberry did not mind that his father was missing. Most of the time his pap had been drunk. When he was sober, he would beat Huck with a stick — if he could catch him. One day a body was found in the river. Everybody said it was Huckleberry's father. The face had been in the water too long to tell for sure.

September came and Huckleberry started to school for the first time in his life. He learned to spell and read and write a little. He could say the multiplication table up to six times seven is thirty-five. He hated school at first, but things got better. Some days he played hooky. The spanking he got always cheered him up.

Snow fell on the ground in late November. One morning

as Huck climbed through the loose board in the garden fence, he jumped with shock. Tracks in the snow! Somebody had stood at the gate. Somebody with a cross in the left boot heel. Huck dropped his schoolbooks and ran as fast as he could across town to Judge Thatcher's house.

"Hello, Huckleberry," said the surprised judge. "What are you doing here so early in the morning? Why, you're all out of breath."

"I want to give you all my money," gasped Huck. "All $6000."

"What for?" asked his friend.

"Don't ask me no questions," said Huck, "so I don't have to tell no lies. Just take it."

Judge Thatcher was not surprised about the money. A year ago Huck and his friend Tom Sawyer found a huge pile of coins that robbers had hidden in a cave. They each got $6000 in gold as a reward, which made them both rich. The kind judge had helped the boys put the money in a bank. Every day they got a dollar apiece to spend as they wished. That was more than either of them knew what to do with.

And now Huckleberry was trying to give it away! The Judge did not want the boy's money, but he knew something was wrong. Huck needed his help.

"I believe you want to *sell* your property to me," said the judge at last. "Here's a dollar in return so it will be legal. Now sign this paper."

Huckleberry signed and breathed a sigh of relief. He knew his money would be safe with his friend.

That night Huckleberry sneaked out of the house to see a black slave named Jim. The man belonged to Miss Watson. He had a hairball as big as a fist that was taken out of an ox's belly. Jim said there was a spirit inside the hairball that knew everything.

"Jim," whispered Huckleberry. "My pap's back. He ain't drowned in the river like everybody says. I saw his tracks in the snow this mornin'."

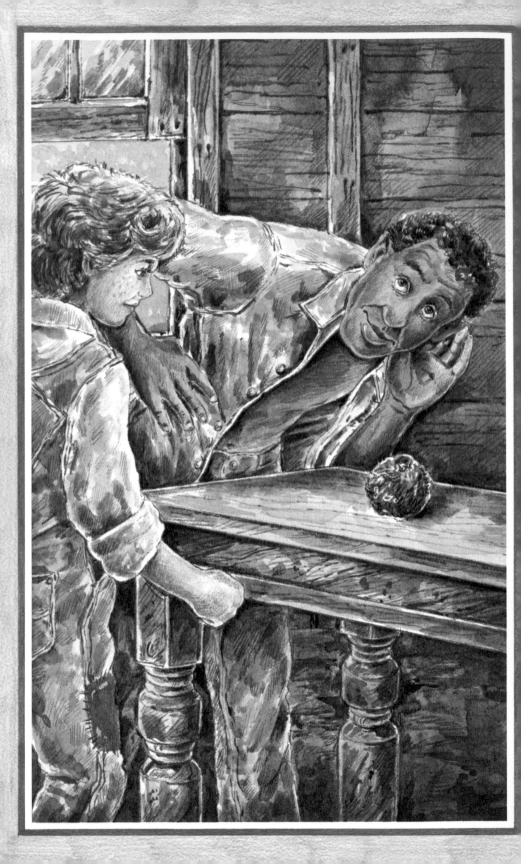

"I'll be," said Jim.

"I want to know if he's gonna stay. What's he gonna do?"

Jim said something over his hairball. He put his ear against it and shook his head.

"It won't talk, Huck," said Jim. "It won't talk sometimes without money."

"I have a fake quarter," offered Huck. He did not tell Jim about his dollar a day.

"Well, maybe that'll do," said Jim. "Maybe the hairball won't know it's no good."

He put the quarter under the hairball and listened again. This time it said that Huck's father did not know what he was going to do. Huck would just have to wait and see.

Huckleberry left the slave's shack and ran back home.He climbed in the window of his bedroom and lit a candle. There on his bed sat Pap!

HUCKLEBERRY'S PAP

2

Huck jumped and backed away toward the door. He was scared of his father. Pap was fifty years old with stringy hair that hung down over his eyes. His face was sickly white like a fish belly. His clothes were in rags. The toes on his right foot stuck out of his broken boot.

"You're wearin' fancy clothes, ain't ya?" sneered Pap. "You think you're a big bug now, don't ya?"

"Maybe I am, maybe I ain't," said Huckleberry.

"Don't give me none of your lip," snapped his father. "Folks tell me you can read and write. You think you're better than your pap, don't ya. Who told you to go to school?"

"The widow did."

"I'll learn her to stick her nose in other people's business. Your mother couldn't read and neither could the rest of your family. If I catch you near that school again, I'll whip you good."

Pap looked at the books on the table. He saw the looking glass on the wall and the carpet on the floor.

"They say you're rich, too," he hissed.

"They lie," answered Huck. "I ain't got no money. Go ask Judge Thatcher. He'll tell you."

"All right, I will. How much you got in your pocket?"

"A dollar, but I want it to . . ."

"Give it to me," snarled Pap. "I ain't had me a drink all day." He grabbed the bill out of Huck's hand and climbed out the window onto the shed. He leaped to the ground and ran down the road toward town.

The next day a drunken Pap went to Judge Thatcher's house and angrily demanded Huck's money. The judge would not give it to him. Pap got even drunker. He went all over town swearing and banging a tin lid. Finally he was put in jail.

"I'm the boss of my son," he yelled. "Someday I'll git that money."

Soon Pap was out of jail. He caught Huckleberry going to school and beat him. Huck went every day after that just to spite his father. One day Pap grabbed Huck and took him in a skiff about three miles up the river. An old log cabin was hidden in the woods. Pap kept Huck in sight every minute. At night he locked the door and put the key under his head. The two fished and hunted for food. Sometimes Pap locked Huckleberry in the hut and went to the store downriver. He traded fish for whiskey. When he came back, he got drunk and beat Huck with a strap.

Except for the beatings, Huck liked his new life. He did not have to study. He could lie around all day fishing. After two months, his clothes were dirty and ragged — just the way he liked them. He did not want to go back to the Widow Douglas and wash every day and eat off a plate.

Pap started getting drunk more often. Huck had welts all over his body from the whippings. One time Pap stabbed at the boy with a knife. Huck sat up all night with a gun across his lap. The next morning when his father was gone, Huckleberry found a rusty wood-saw in the rafters of the hut. He sawed at the planks on the floor beneath the table. When he saw Pap coming, he hid the saw in the rafters again.

"Git up!" yelled his father with a kick. "Go see if there's a fish on the line. I'll be there in a minute."

Huckleberry ran to the riverbank. The water had risen during the night. Logs and branches floated down the stream. Suddenly an empty canoe came drifting along.

Huck caught the boat and hid it in the bushes where his father could not see it.

"What's taking you so long?" yelled Pap.

"I fell in the river," called Huck. "That's why I'm so wet."

"Let's git some of these logs here, boy. I can sell them in town."

By noontime, nine logs were dragged ashore. Pap locked Huck in the cabin and went downstream in the skiff filled with logs. Huck took the saw out again. Before long he had cut a hole through the floor and crawled out from the hut. He filled a blanket with pots and pans, food, fishlines, matches, a gun and bullets. Quickly he loaded the goods in the hidden canoe. He replaced the sawed-off plank and covered up his tracks to the boat.

Huck hunted in the woods until he shot a wild pig. He carried it back to the cabin and slashed its throat. With the ax he smashed in the door of the hut. Then he dragged the pig to the river and flung it in.

"They'll follow that blood to the water and think I was killed and drowned," Huck said to himself.

By this time darkness had fallen. Huckleberry took the canoe downriver to some willow trees and tied up. He lay down to wait for moonlight. Before long he was fast asleep.

Huck woke with a start. It was late. He had not meant to sleep. He was bending over the canoe to untie it when he heard the sound of paddles. A skiff was coming across the water.

"That's Pap," said Huck, frightened. "I didn't think he'd be back tonight."

The next minute Huck was floating downstream in the shade of the bank. He lay in the bottom of the canoe and looked at the cloudless sky. Soon he was at Jackson's Island, a lonely place where a boy could hide. Huckleberry hid the boat and slept till dawn.

THE RUNAWAY

3

All morning Huck lay at the edge of the island and watched the ferryboat through the bushes. Pap and Judge Thatcher and many others were looking for his body.

When the boat finally left, Huck made a tent out of blankets. He caught a catfish for supper. Three days and nights he stayed right there. The fourth day he took his gun to kill some game. Suddenly Huck came upon a smoking campfire. His heart leaped into his mouth! He had thought he was all alone on the island. Quickly Huck slipped back to his tent. He jammed his belongings into the canoe, scattered the ashes of his fire, and climbed a tree. By night-time he was very tired and hungry.

"I've got to find out who is on this island," thought Huckleberry. "I can't live in fear the rest of my life."

When he found the other campfire he stopped still. Someone was lying on the ground asleep. Huck sat on a log pointing his gun until the man moved. It was Miss Watson's black slave, Jim!

"Hey, Jim!" shouted Huck happily. "Am I glad to see you."

Jim leaped up and stared wildly. He dropped on his knees and put his hands together in prayer.

"Don't hurt me, Huckleberry. Please don't hurt me. I ain't never done no harm to no ghost. I always liked dead people. You go git in the river where you belongs."

"I ain't dead," laughed Huckleberry. "I faked that whole

thing. I wanted to git away from my pap and not have to go back to the Widow Douglas neither."

"Why are you here, Jim?" asked Huckleberry.

"Maybe I better not tell," replied Jim. "You wouldn't tell on me, would ya, Huck?"

"Course not," answered the boy.

"Well, Huck Finn, I'm runnin' away. Miss Watson, she's always pickin' on me. Then the other night I heerd her tell the Widow Douglas she was gonna sell me to a slave trader for $800. I lit out mighty fast, I tell ya."

"What you gonna do now, Jim?" asked Huck.

"I don't know. But nobody's gonna own me no more. I owns myself. I's worth $800. I only wisht I had the money."

Huckleberry and Jim found a big cavern in the rock at the top of a hill. They hid the canoe and carried all Huck's goods into their new home. One time after a bad storm a whole cabin came downstream. Jim waded out and climbed aboard. He came back with clothes and candles.

After a while, Huckleberry grew tired of the island. He decided to slip upriver and find out what was going on back home.

"I'll have to go at night so nobody'll know me," said Huck.

"Why don't you dress up like a girl?" suggested Jim. "We got some cotton gowns in that stuff from the river."

Huck turned up his pant legs and pulled a dress over his head. He tied on a sunbonnet. All day he practiced being a girl. When it was dark he rowed his canoe to the edge of town. A light was burning in an old cabin that used to be empty. Inside Huck could see a woman he did not know. He knocked at the door.

"Come in," called the woman. Huck stepped inside. "Take a chair. What's your name?"

"Sarah Williams," replied Huckleberry in a high squeaky voice.

"Do you live around here?" asked the woman, looking at him closely.

"No, ma'am. I live seven miles away. I walked the whole way. My ma's sick and I come to tell my uncle in town."

"Why it's a long ways to town yet and it's dark. Why don't you stay here tonight?"

"Thank you, ma'am, but I'll just stay a minute to rest. I ain't afraid of the dark."

The woman told him she had just moved to town with her husband. Before long she was telling him about pap and the murder of a boy named Huckleberry Finn.

"Who done it?" asked Huck.

"Well, some folks think his own father done it," she replied. "But then Miss Watson's Jim run away the same night, so most others say he done it."

"Why no, he . . ." Huck started to say, then stopped.

"There's a reward out for him of $300," the woman went on. "I think the runaway's over on Jackson Island. I'm sure I seen smoke there a couple of days ago. My husband's going over there at midnight with a friend to look around."

Huck grabbed a needle off the table and tried to thread it. His hands shook all over. The woman looked at him strangely.

"What did you say your name was, Honey?" she asked.

"Mary — Mary Williams," stammered Huck.

"Come, now. What's your real name? Is it Bill or Tom or Bob? You're not a girl, that's for sure. You're a runaway apprentice, aren't you?" she said. "It's all right. I won't turn you in."

"Thank you kindly, ma'am," said Huck with relief. "I guess I'd better git movin'. My ma's awful sick."

As soon as he was out of the cabin, Huck fled to the canoe. He paddled as hard as he could to the island.

"Jim, Jim! Git up! There ain't a minute to lose. They're after us," yelled Huckleberry.

Without a word the black man grabbed their belongings and carried them to the raft they had made. Huck tied on the canoe and the two slid away from the island and down the Mississippi River.

TROUBLE IN THE NIGHT

4

The runaways saw no one the whole night. At daybreak they hid their raft and watched the boats go by. When night came, Jim took planks from one end of the raft and built a wigwam in the center to keep them dry. He put six inches of dirt in the middle to build a fire on. Huck hung a lantern on a pole so steamboats could see them in the dark. The two started downriver again. They caught fish to eat and lay on their backs looking up at the stars. On the fifth night they passed St. Louis. It looked like the whole world was lit up. There were 30,000 people living there. Huck and Jim could not believe the sight.

Sometimes Huckleberry slipped ashore and bought cornmeal and coffee. Sometimes he borrowed a watermelon from a farmer's patch. The two shot water birds for meat. Huck thought it was a most wonderful life.

"Three more nights, Jim, and we should be at Cairo, Illinois. That's where the Ohio River comes in," said Huckleberry.

"What do we do then, Huck?" asked Jim.

"Well, we'll sell the raft. Then we'll have the money to get on a steamboat up the Ohio River to the free states. By that time we'll be out of trouble for sure."

"That sounds mighty good to this ole black man," sighed Jim. They floated downriver for a long while without seeing a light. Jim was trembling all over to be so close to freedom.

"If we git to Cairo I's a free man," he said over and over. "But if we miss it, I'll still be in slave country."

Huckleberry began to tremble, too. If Jim did get free, Huck was to blame. He was helping a runaway slave escape. He could be put in jail for years. Jim belonged to Miss Watson. Huckleberry had no right to steal what was hers. Jim was worth $800. Huck decided he would be doing the right thing if he turned Jim in at the next town.

"Know the first thing I'm gonna do when I's free, Huck?" asked Jim. Huckleberry did not answer.

"I's gonna save up every cent I can earn and buy my wife. Then we'll both work and buy our two chillen. If their owner won't sell 'em I'll just go *steal* 'em."

Huckleberry sat frozen. Jim would never have dared talk like that before. See what comes of helping a slave? They start thinking they're as good as the next person.

"There's Cairo. I know it is!" sang out Jim. "I's as good as free. It's all because of you, Huck. Without you I'd have never done it. You's the best friend I ever had."

Huck got in the canoe and paddled off. His hands were clammy and his throat hurt. Soon two men came alongside the canoe.

"What's over there?" asked one of the men.

"A raft," said Huck.

"Any men on it?"

"Just one, sir" answered Huck.

"Well, we're looking for five slaves that run off tonight. Is your man white or black?"

Huck tried to answer right out, but the words stuck in his throat. Finally he mumbled, "He's white, sir."

"We'll just go see for ourselves," said the other man.

"I sure wish you would," said Huck quickly. "It's my father and he's awful sick. So's my mother and sister. Nobody I ask will come help us."

"Don't come any closer, boy," said the man. "You just stay back. Your family's got smallpox, ain't they?"

Huckleberry started to cry. Sobs shook his body.

"Please help us," he begged. "Everybody else just rowed away. What am I gonna do?"

"We'd sure like to help you, son," said the man, "but we don't want to catch smallpox. You go on down about twenty miles to the next town. You can get help there. Here's some money to pay for it." He tossed Huck two twenty dollar gold pieces.

"Thank you, sir," called out Huck. As soon as the men left, Huck rowed back to the raft.

"Lordy, how you fooled them, Huckleberry. I heerd every word you said," said Jim happily.

Huck gave the black man one of the gold pieces and kept one. The money was enough to buy them passage on a steamboat as far as they wanted to go. That night the two saw town after town, but none of them was Cairo.

"Jim, we must have passed it in the fog the other night," said Huck sadly. "We've gone too far."

The fog rolled in again so thick they could not see each other. Soon they heard the puffing noise of a steamboat. It was coming right at them!

"Jump, Jim!" yelled Huck as he dived over the side. The steamboat smashed right through the raft. Huck swam to the bottom to escape the paddle wheel. His lungs were bursting for air. He grabbed a floating plank when he came up and pushed for shore. Panting heavily, he climbed up the bank. Not far away was a huge log house. Dogs howled and barked. Huckleberry froze in his path.

"Quiet, dogs!" yelled a voice from inside the house. "Who's out there?"

"It's just me," answered Huckleberry in a frightened tone.

"What's your name?"

"George Jackson," lied Huck.

"What do you want?"

"Nothin', sir. I just want to go along, but the dogs won't let me," said Huck.

"What are you snooping around this time of night for?"

"I ain't snoopin', sir. I fell off a steamboat and swum to shore."

"All right, young man. If you're telling the truth, there's nothing to fear. Step inside. Open the door yourself."

Huckleberry inched forward. All he could hear was the thumping in his chest. The dogs followed closely behind. He pushed the door open and stuck his head inside. Three large men stood with guns pointing right at him. Behind them sat a gray-haired lady and two beautiful young women.

"Well," said the older man. "I guess everything's all right. Come on in." He barred and bolted the door. They went into the parlor out of range of the windows. The men searched Huckleberry for weapons before giving him a chair.

"I'm Colonel Grangerford. We thought you might be a Sheperdson, but I can see you're not," explained the older man.

Mrs. Grangerford got Huckleberry some dry clothes and a meal. She woke her thirteen-year-old son Buck. The whole family sat around the table smoking corncob pipes, even the women. The house was the biggest and prettiest Huckleberry had ever seen. A big brick fireplace stood at one end of the parlor. A fancy clock sat on the mantel. Carpeting covered the floor. There were china dishes and lace tablecloths.

The Grangerfords invited Huckleberry to stay with them as long as he wanted. Huck could see that the colonel was a high-born gentleman. Every day he wore a clean shirt and white suit and carried a silver-handled cane. His sons bowed to him and said, "Good morning to you, sir." Each person in the family had a black slave, even Huckleberry. The colonel owned many farms and over 100 slaves. Sometimes there were dances and picnics. People came from many miles and stayed five or six days.

The Shepherdsons were another family in the area. They were just as rich. For over thirty years the two families

had been fighting. Each Grangerford man killed a Shepherdson whenever he could, and vice versa. Nobody went anywhere without a gun.

Huckleberry was happy staying with the Grangerfords. Buck was as good a friend as Tom Sawyer. They shared the same bed and clothes and spent many hours together.

One day when Buck was off with his brothers, Huckleberry went down by the river to look for snakes. He waded across a swamp and found an open place the size of a bedroom. Vines hung all about hiding it from view. On the ground lay a man asleep.

"Jim!" Huck yelled "You're alive! Man, I thought you drowned in the river."

The black man was glad to see Huck, but not surprised. He had swum behind the boy after the raft was struck. He heard Huckleberry call to him, but did not answer. He was afraid of being picked up and sent back to slavery. When Jim reached shore, he ran for the woods. The next day a Grangerford slave found him hiding in the trees and took him to the open place. Each day he brought water and food and news about Huckleberry.

"I been patchin' up our old raft, Huck," said Jim.

"You mean it weren't smashed to bits?"

"No, sir. It was tore up a good bit, but I saved a lot of the stuff. Now she's good as new."

"That's grand, Jim," said Huckleberry. "I gotta go now, but I'll be back to see you."

THE SHOOTOUT

5

When Huckleberry woke up the next morning, the house was deathly still. Buck was gone and there was nobody around. Outside Huckleberry saw his slave boy, Jack.

"What's happening?" asked Huck.

"Miss Sophie Grangerford's run off in the night with one of them Shepherdson boys. They're gittin' married. All the men took off with horses and guns. The women folk went to get help. If they catch that boy, they'll kill him for sure."

Huck ran up the river as fast as he could. He heard the sounds of guns in the distance. Quickly he climbed a cottonwood tree to look around. Soon young Buck and his cousin Tom came tearing down the road, swearing and crying.

"What's happened, Buck?" called Huck from the tree.

The boy sobbed that Sophie and her lover had got safely across the river. Shepherdsons had killed Colonel Grangerford and Buck's two brothers. Just then three or four guns went off at Buck and Tom. The boys leaped for the river. Both were badly hurt. Shepherdsons ran along the bank still shooting.

"Kill them! Kill them!" shouted the men.

Huckleberry could see it all from the tree. He wished he had not come ashore that night. Never before had he felt so sick. He stayed in the cottonwood until dark, afraid to come down. At last he jumped down and crawled along the bank to the boys' bodies. He dragged them from the water and covered their faces with branches, crying as he covered Buck's. Then he crept toward the swamp where Jim was hiding.

The black man grabbed and hugged him. "Bless you chile. I thought you was dead and gone. I got the raft ready and was just waitin' here just in case. I's mighty glad you's alive, boy."

Huckleberry sobbed out the story of what he had seen. "Everybody will think I'm dead, too, Jim. Let's just shove off for the big water as fast as we can. I won't feel easy till we're out in the middle of the Mississippi."

Three days went by very quietly. The runaways floated at night and hid during the day. They fished and swam and slept and listened to the stillness. Sometimes they had the whole big river to themselves.

One morning Huckleberry took the canoe and paddled up a creek to hunt for berries. Suddenly two men came running toward him.

"Please help us," they called. "They're after us and we ain't done nothing." Huckleberry could hear other men and dogs coming down the path.

"Git in," he said.

They climbed aboard and Huck rowed down the creek to the raft. The men were dressed in greasy coats and ragged jeans. The older one was bald with gray whiskers.

"Who are you?" asked Huckleberry.

"I'm the Duke of Bridgewater," replied the younger man. Jim's eyes bugged out when he heard that.

"My great-grandfather came to this country for freedom and lost his rightful title. My family has been poor ever since," said the man. Tears flowed from his eyes. Jim and Huck felt sorry for the poor man who should be rich.

"You want to know who I am?" asked the bald-headed one. "I'm the true king of France." He started to cry, too. Huck and Jim bowed to the men and called them "Your Majesty" and waited on them hand and foot.

Before long, however, Huck decided the men were not

royalty at all but crooks and liars. He said nothing to Jim, for he wanted to keep peace on the raft.

"Is he a runaway slave?" asked the king about Jim.

"Oh, no," lied Huck. "Would a runaway be heading South? He belonged to my poor pap who drowned, so now he's *my* man."

Huck soon learned how the newcomers earned a living. The king sold poems he made up, ads to a fake newspaper, or medicine that cleaned your teeth and cured cancer at the same time. The duke was a self-taught actor who did scenes from Shakespeare plays. Other times he preached at camp meetings. Each time he passed a hat for money. One night he collected $85. Most of it was spent on whiskey.

When the king, duke, and Huck went ashore to work the towns, they dressed Jim up in a costume with a white wig and beard. They painted his face a dull blue with make-up. He looked like a man who had been drowned for nine days. The duke painted a sign that said:

Sick Arab — but harmless when not out of his head

When anybody came near, Jim stepped out of the wigwam, beat his chest and howled. Nobody bothered him.

One day the king and duke heard about a rich man who had just died. He had three teenage daughters who were now orphans. He also had two brothers living in England whom the girls had never seen. The man left a will giving part of his estate to the daughters and part to the brothers.

The king and duke dressed up in good clothes. Talking in a fake English accent, they went to the dead man's house and claimed to be his brothers. Huckleberry went with them. The crooks cried over the body and kissed the girls.

When the will was read the next day, the two men received a bag of $6000 in gold pieces and some of the property. They hid the gold under the mattress in their bedroom. As soon as the man was buried and the property sold, they planned to run away with the money.

Huckleberry felt sorry for the girls and thought the

money should be theirs. He sneaked into the bedroom and stole the bag of coins. Wondering what to do with the money, he slipped inside the parlor where the body was lying. When he heard footsteps coming, he stuffed the bag inside the coffin.

The funeral was held that afternoon. Huck watched closely as the box was lowered in the grave. No one had seen the money.

"Good," thought Huck. "When I git away I'll send a letter to the girls and tell them where the gold is. They can dig up the coffin and keep the money for themselves."

That evening the duke and king discovered the gold was gone. They cornered Huck in the hallway.

"Were you in our room, Huckleberry?" asked the king.

"No, sir," he lied.

"Did you see anyone go in?"

"Just the man who made up the beds. The one they sold yesterday to the slave trader," said Huck.

The king let go of Huck's shirt. With the $6000 gone, the only thing to do was sell the rest of the property as soon as possible. Huckleberry felt very proud. He had stolen back the gold for the girls and the crooks believed his lie about the slave.

ESCAPE

6

The next evening, a crowd gathered at the house. All the property was to be sold. Suddenly two strange men drove up in a carriage.

"I'm Harvey Wilk and this is my brother, William," said the old man in an English accent. "We came for my brother's funeral."

"They're fakes!" yelled the duke. "They're just after the money." The crowd gathered around. There was shouting back and forth between the stranger and the duke. Finally someone asked, "Which of you can prove the dead man's your brother?"

"He had a blue arrow on his chest," guessed the king.

"No, he didn't" said the stranger. "He had the letters P and W."

"Let's go dig him up!" shouted a voice. The crowd roared and started off toward the graveyard. Huckleberry felt someone hold tightly to his arm as they ran. He knew if the duke and king were jailed, he would be too. Dirt sailed out of the grave as the men dug away. At last the coffin was reached and the lid pried off.

"By jingo! Here's a bag of gold on his chest!" a man called out. The crowd rushed forward. Huckleberry's arm was free. In a split second, he was off down the road. Nobody saw him in the dark. He raced through the town toward the river. Finding an unchained canoe, he shoved off.

"Let her loose, Jim!" he called when he reached the raft. "We're rid of them."

Jim came grinning towards him with both arms out. Huck screamed and fell backwards into the water. He had forgotten about Jim's costume and blue face.

"You scared the daylights out of me," Huck shouted. Jim fished him out of the water, then let the raft slide out into the river. Huck skipped around on the planks.

"Whoopee!" he yelled. "We're free again. Just the two of us."

Suddenly Huck stopped short. He sank down on the planks with his head in his arms and cried.

Coming right at them on a skiff were the king and the duke!

"We'll git away from them as soon as we can, Jim," whispered Huckleberry the following morning. The next time the crooks went ashore, Huck went too. At the first chance he ran like a deer back to the raft.

"Jim! Jim! Where are you?" he called. There was no answer. The black man was gone. Huck saw a boy on the road and called from the raft.

"Have you seen a man dressed up in a costume with a blue face?" he asked.

"Yeah," said the boy. "He's a runaway slave. Two men just gave him to Mr. Phelps for the reward."

Huck felt very bad. After all the trouble they had been through, Jim was going to be a slave again. And not even at home near his wife and children.

"I'll just have to steal him back," said Huckleberry at last. He took the raft downriver and hid it. He put on good clothes and took the canoe to shore. After loading it with rocks, he sank it in the water where it could be found if needed.

Before long, Huck found a large house with a sign that said, "Phelps Sawmill." He went around to the kitchen door. Dogs barked from everywhere. Out the door came a middle-aged woman.

"It's you at last, ain't it?" she said.

"Yes'm," said Huckleberry without thinking.

The woman hugged him tight with tears in her eyes. "You don't look as much like your mother as I thought you would, but that don't matter. I'm so glad to see you."

She led Huck toward the house. "We've been expecting you for days. Did the boat run aground?"

"Yes'm," answered Huck.

"Don't say yes'm — say Aunt Sally."

Huckleberry was very uneasy. Who was he supposed to be? He opened his mouth to tell her the truth when Mr. Phelps drove up in a wagon. He had gone to town to meet the boat again, but it still had not come.

"Who's that?" he asked when he saw Huckleberry.

"Why, it's Tom. Tom Sawyer!" said Mrs. Phelps.

Huckleberry almost went through the ground. Now he knew who he was! Being Tom Sawyer would be as easy as pie. He could tell all they wanted to know and more.

Suddenly a steamboat blew its horn on the river. Huckleberry jumped a mile. What if the real Tom Sawyer was on that boat? He told the folks he had to go down for his baggage. If Tom were there, Huck would have to get to him fast.

RESCUE

7

Huckleberry started for town in the Phelps' wagon. Halfway there he met Tom Sawyer coming towards him. Tom's mouth fell open and his eyes bugged out.

"I ain't never done you no harm," he cried. "Why you comin' back to haunt me?"

Huckleberry laughed. "I ain't no ghost. Honest injun."

"You mean you wasn't never murdered?"

"Nope. Come feel me." Huck stuck out an arm. Then he told Tom the fix he was in. He knew his old friend would think of something.

"You take my trunk of clothes," Tom said at last. "I'll show up a little later."

"All right," said Huck. "But there's somethin' else. I'm trying to steal Miss Watson's Jim out of slavery."

"What!" cried Tom. "Why, Jim . . ." He stopped short and looked at Huck.

"I know you think it's wrong, but I'm gonna do it anyways," said Huck. "I just don't want ya to tell."

Tom's eyes lit up. "Sure, Huck. I'll even help you."

"You're jokin'." He could not believe a well-brought-up boy like Tom Sawyer would stoop to stealing a slave.

Huckleberry took the trunk and drove back to the Phelps' place. Some time later Tom arrived. He told Aunt Sally that he was Sid Sawyer, Tom's cousin.

"Oh, dear. What a surprise!" cried Aunt Sally. She hugged and kissed him. "We didn't know *you* were coming, too."

Tom and Huck were shown the room they were to share. After dark, they sneaked out the bedroom window and found Jim locked inside a small hut. Huckleberry wanted to steal the key and get the black man right out.

"That's too easy," said Tom. "It wouldn't give folks anything to talk about."

"Then what'll we do?"

"We'll dig him out. We'll make a tunnel under the hut and saw through the floor. It'll take at least a week."

The next morning the boys went with a Phelps' slave to give Jim his food. Tom slipped over to the runaway and whispered, "If you hear digging, don't worry. We're gonna set you free."

When they got back to the house, Tom said, "We've got to make a rope ladder."

"Whatever for?" asked Huck. "The hut's only one story."

"Because that's the way it's always done," snapped Tom. "We can take it to him in a pie."

"Want to use those old broken picks in the shed to dig him out with?" asked Huckleberry.

"Huck Finn, you are so dumb. You might as well just give Jim the key. What we need is knives."

"Knives! To dig a tunnel? That'll take years!"

"So what," snorted Tom. When the household was asleep, the boys sneaked to the hut. They dug till after midnight, but barely made a dent in the ground. Blisters stung their hands.

"I guess it ain't gonna work, Huck," said Tom at last. "It ain't right, but we'll have to use picks after all."

Many nights passed as they chipped away underneath Jim's hut. One day they took a huge bag of flour to the woods. They tore a sheet into strips, which they tied into a ladder and baked in a giant pie. They slipped it to Jim to hide under his mattress.

"You need some spiders and snakes and rats in here, too," said Tom.

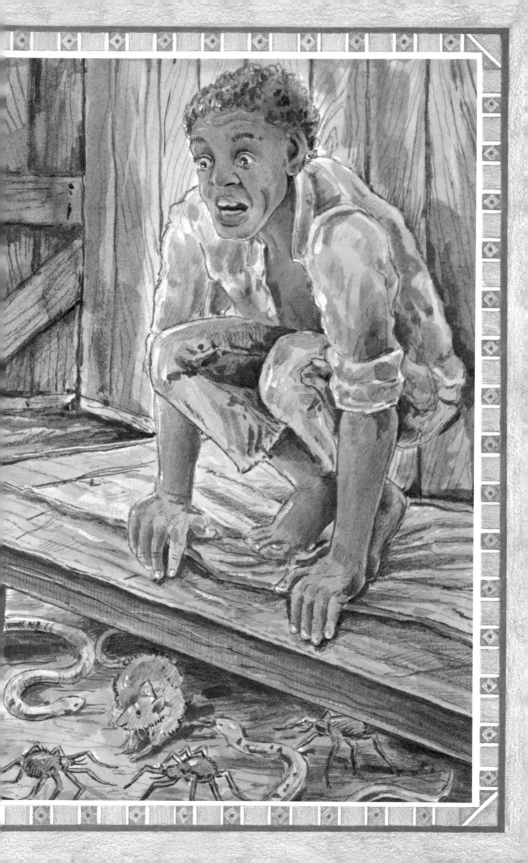

"Oh, Lordy, Tom!" cried Jim. "I's skeered of them things."

"You gotta have them. It's always the way," said Tom.

The next morning Huck and Tom found a rat-trap and caught fifteen large rats. They hunted for spiders and snakes and set them all loose in Jim's little hut.

"I'd ruther be a slave than a prisoner," complained Jim. "With everything bitin' all the time, a body can't git no sleep."

After three weeks, Tom decided it was time to free Jim. That night he stuck a note on the Phelps' front door. It said that a gang of murderers was going to steal the runaway slave. Farmers from all around came to the house with guns. Tom was thrilled.

The boys slipped out the window and ran to the hut. They crawled through the tunnel and rescued Jim just as the men opened the cabin door. The three raced toward the river and Huck's hidden canoe. Guns blazed after them! They climbed in the boat and rowed to the island where the raft was tied.

"That was beautiful!" exclaimed Tom.

"What's wrong with your leg?" asked Huckleberry. "Why, it's bleedin'."

"Oh, it ain't much," said Tom through his teeth. A bullet was stuck in his calf. Jim said they had to get a doctor. He stopped the blood with rags while Huck climbed back into the canoe.

"Be sure to blindfold the doctor," called Tom weakly. "That's the way it's always done."

Huckleberry found a kind old doctor. He told the man that he and his younger brother had gone to the island to camp and hunt. The kid had shot himself in the leg by accident.

"This canoe's too small for both of us," said the doctor. "You'll have to stay here. I'll go by myself."

Huckleberry did not like the idea, but he knew Tom needed help. He lay down to rest until the doctor came

back. Soon he was sound asleep. In the morning Mr. Phelps found Huck still sleeping and took him back to the house. Aunt Sally kissed him and asked about Sid.

"Oh, he'll be along. He's still lookin' for the runaway," lied Huck. He did not tell her about the bullet in Tom's leg.

A shout was heard from outside! Down the path came the doctor and other men carrying Tom on a mattress. Behind walked Jim with his hands tied.

All day and night Tom lay in bed with a fever. The next morning he awoke in good spirits. Before Huck could stop him, Tom told Aunt Sally proudly about Jim's rescue. When he learned that Jim was chained up again he cried out.

"That ain't right! You turn him loose this minute."

"Whatever do you mean?" asked Aunt Sally.

"Cause he's a free man. Miss Watson died two months ago. She set Jim free in her will."

"You mean you've known this all along! Why didn't you just tell us instead of trying to dig him out?"

"If that doesn't sound just like a woman," snapped Tom. "That's not the way they do it in the books."

Suddenly another woman was standing in the doorway. Huck took one look and dived under the bed.

"Aunt Polly!" exclaimed Tom Sawyer.

"What on earth have you been up to, Tom?" scolded the woman.

"Why, Sis," said Aunt Sally. "That's not Tom in bed. That's Sid. Tom's over . . . where did he go?"

"You mean that rascal, Huck Finn," snorted Aunt Polly. "You come out from under that bed this minute, young man."

Huckleberry slowly crawled out. He felt bad when he saw how confused Aunt Sally was. He explained why he had pretended to be Tom and Tom to be Sid.

"I just wanted to git Jim loose," he said.

Aunt Polly agreed that Miss Watson had freed Jim. Suddenly Huck understood why Tom had been so willing to help him steal a slave. He knew Jim was already free.

The Phelps unchained Jim. They gave him food and clothes and praised him for helping Tom. When he and the boys were alone, Tom gave the black man forty dollars for being such a good prisoner. Jim was very proud and happy.

"You still got your $6000, Huck," said Tom. "Your pap never came back for it."

Jim was silent for a minute. "There's somethin' I didn't tell ya, Huck. 'Member that cabin we seen floatin' down the river when we was on Jackson Island? Your pap was in it. Shot in the back. The money's all yours. He ain't never comin' back."

Huckleberry said good-bye to his old friends. Then he slipped out of the house and down the road. Aunt Sally had said she wanted him to stay and be her son, just like the Widow Douglas. Huck knew he would have to wear clean clothes and say his prayers and go to school again. Maybe he'd go West. He had to get away fast, before they civilized him.

GLOSSARY

apprentice   (ə prent′ əs)   a person who learns a skill by working for a skilled worker

civilize   (siv′ ə līz)   to raise someone from a savage or ignorant condition

royalty   (roi′ əl tē)   people who belong to the family of kings and queens

skiff   (skif)   a small rowboat

smallpox   (smȯl′ päks′)   a disease that spreads easily, leaving spots on the skin

steamboat   (stēm′ bōt′)   a boat, usually large, moved by steam